# ACTIVATE

## AUGMENTED REALITY

# CONTENTS

The Rise and Fall of Anakin Skywalker – **6**

Episode I: *The Phantom Menace* – **8**

Jedi Knights: Protectors of the Peace – **16**

Episode II: *Attack of the Clones* – **18**

Droid Search – **26**

Droid Class – **27**

Episode III: *Revenge of the Sith* – **28**

Death Star: The Ultimate Weapon – **36**

The Jedi Path – **38**

Episode IV: *A New Hope* – **40**

*Millennium Falcon*: The Fastest Hunk of Junk in the Galaxy – **48**

Episode V: *The Empire Strikes Back* – **50**

Sith Lords: Ancient Order of the Dark Side – **58**

Episode VI: *Return of the Jedi* – **60**

Answer Pages – **68**

# STAR WARS ™

## AUGMENTED REALITY INSTRUCTIONS:

Download the free Star Wars Annual 2015 app from the App Store or Google Play Store to your phone or tablet. Open the app, tap the play button and hold your device close to the Stormtrooper Marker (inside the front cover), ensuring the image fits within the screen.

To spin the Death Star simply run your finger across the screen, and tap to stop. You can change to hologram mode by tapping on the yellow Death Star icon. To destroy the Death Star, tap on the explosion icon, which will begin the countdown.

Note: for best results, ensure you are positioned in good light and that there are no shadows or objects between your device and the marker image.

## EGMONT
*We bring stories to life*

First published in Great Britain 2014 by Egmont UK Limited
The Yellow Building, 1 Nicholas Road, London W11 4AN
Written by Gemma Lowe and Katrina Pallant
Designed by Richie Hull
Cover Design by Maddox Philpot
Illustrated by Dan Crisp

© 2014 Lucasfilm Ltd. & ™.
ISBN 978 1 4052 7212 4
57519/1
Printed in Italy

# THE RISE AND FALL OF
# ANAKIN SKYWALKER

**BBY** = Before the Battle of Yavin

**ABY** = After the Battle of Yavin

## 32 BBY

A young Anakin Skywalker is discovered on Tatooine by two Jedi Knights. He is believed to be the Chosen One who will return balance to the Force.

## 22-19 BBY

The Clone Wars were started, maintained and eventually ended by the Dark Lord of the Sith, Darth Sidious. He wanted to rule over a galactic empire and eradicate the Jedi Order.

Anakin becomes a Jedi Knight and forms a close friendship with Palpatine, the Supreme Chancellor of the Republic.

**EPISODE I**
THE PHANTOM MENACE

**EPISODE II**
ATTACK OF THE CLONES

**EPISODE III**
REVENGE OF THE SITH

## 19 BBY

Anakin kills Count Dooku, a former Jedi Master who has fallen to the dark side.

Obi-Wan severely wounds and defeats Darth Vader in a duel.

Palpatine is revealed to be Darth Sidious. He declares himself Emperor and coaxes Anakin to the dark side.

Senator Amidala gives birth to twins, Luke and Leia Skywalker.

## 22 BBY

Anakin returns home after training as Obi-Wan's Padawan to find his mother has been killed. His anger and grief leads him to murder an entire village of Tusken Raiders.

Anakin is tasked with protecting Senator Amidala from assassins. The two fall in love and marry in secret.

Anakin becomes Darth Vader and helps his new Master dissolve the Jedi Order.

Obi-Wan hides Luke on Tatooine and Leia with Senator Bail Organa to keep them safe from Darth Sidious.

## BATTLE OF YAVIN

One of the Rebellion's first victories, the Battle of Yavin, was a major event in the Galactic Civil War.

### 3 ABY

The Empire attacks the Rebel base on Hoth.

Vader plans to capture and convert Luke to the dark side.

Palpatine tells Vader that Luke is his son and it was he who blew up the Death Star.

Darth Vader cuts off Luke Skywalker's hand and reveals to Luke that he is his father.

### EPISODE IV
A NEW HOPE

### EPISODE V
THE EMPIRE STRIKES BACK

### EPISODE VI
RETURN OF THE JEDI

**0 ABY**

### 0 BBY

Plans for the most dangerous Imperial weapon, the Death Star, are stolen by Princess Leia and the Rebel Alliance but she is captured in flight by Darth Vader.

The Death Star blows up Alderaan.

Darth Vader kills his old master, Obi-Wan Kenobi.

Luke joins Obi-Wan to get the plans to the Alliance. He trains to be a Jedi just like his father. Obi-Wan gives Luke his father's lightsaber.

With the assistance of Han Solo, Luke defeats Darth Vader and destroys the Death Star during the battle of Yavin.

### 4 ABY

Luke Skywalker reveals to Leia that they are brother and sister, and that Darth Vader is their father. He goes alone to confront the Sith.

Darth Vader destroys Palpatine, saving his son's life, and dies on the light side.

Luke duels with Darth Vader and Vader is finally redeemed to the light side.

The prophecy of the Chosen One is fulfilled as he brings balance to the Force.

# WELCOME TO THE GALACTIC REPUBLIC

It was a time of turmoil across the thousands of worlds of the Galactic Republic, including the small and peaceful planet of Naboo. The greedy Trade Federation stopped all shipping with a blockade of deadly battleships, demanding more money. The Galactic Senate sent two Jedi Knights, the guardians of peace and order, to negotiate: Jedi Master Qui-Gon Jinn and his young apprentice Obi-Wan Kenobi.

"I have a bad feeling about this," said Obi-Wan, as they waited in the Trade Federation ship.

"Don't centre on your anxieties, Obi-Wan. Keep your concentration here and now where it belongs," warned his teacher Qui-Gon.

But meanwhile, Viceroy Nute Gunray, the head of the Trade Federation, was speaking to his secret ally, the evil Sith Lord Darth Sidious. Sidious's plan was to invade Naboo. The Jedi ambassadors, he said, must be killed before they could interfere.

**"BE MINDFUL OF THE LIVING FORCE."**
QUI-GON JINN

Gunray gave orders to have the Jedi Knights' ship destroyed, and the room they were in filled with poison gas – but when battle droids opened the door to check that they were dead, Qui-Gon and Obi-Wan stepped out, lightsabers drawn, and fought them all.

Qui-Gon then tried to get access to the main deck, where the Viceroy was hiding, by burning through the door with his lightsaber, but before he could get through they were ambushed by droidekas – robots with powerful shield generators. The Jedi were forced to retreat.

In the hangar bay, Qui-Gon spotted the Trade Federation's army of battle droids preparing to land. "We've got to warn Naboo. Let's split up, board separate ships and meet down on the planet," said Qui-Gon.

# STAR-DOKU

Can you fill the pictures into the grid below so there's only one of each picture in each row and column and box?

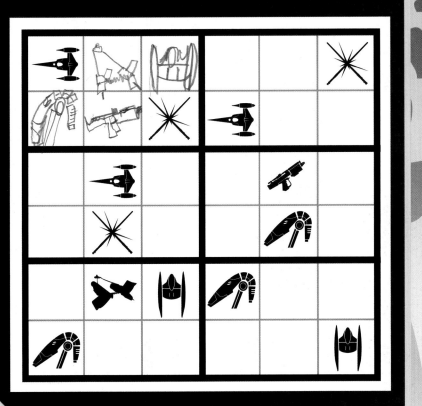

# "I LOVE YOU!"

On the surface of Naboo, Qui-Gon saves the life of a Gungan. The pictures below are clues to this Gungan's name – what is it?

# INVASION OF NABOO

**W**hen Qui-Gon, Obi-Wan and their Gungan guide Jar Jar Binks arrived in Naboo city, the Trade Federation army had already invaded, capturing Naboo's Queen Amidala. The Viceroy wanted the Queen to sign a treaty, making the invasion legal.

"I will not cooperate," said the Queen.

"The suffering of your people will persuade you to see our point of view," replied the Viceroy.

As the royal party were led outside the palace, Qui-Gon and Obi-Wan attacked. They swiftly cut down the Federation's battle droids and rescued the Queen.

"We are ambassadors for the Supreme Chancellor," Qui-Gon explained. "We need to contact the Senate immediately."

The Trade Federation had knocked out Naboo's communication, so the Jedi needed to escape to Coruscant – the home planet of the

## "THEY WILL KILL YOU IF YOU STAY."
#### OBI-WAN KENOBI

Republic, and where the Galactic Senate met. They made their way to the hangar bay.

"Your highness, in the circumstances, I suggest you come with us. They will kill you if you stay," said Obi-Wan.

"My place is with my people," said the Queen. "But I will plead our case to the Senate."

The Queen and her party escaped Naboo and flew into space. As they approached the Trade Federation blockade they were attacked, and though a special droid called R2-D2 fixed the damage, the hyperdrive generator was broken. They decided to land on a planet called Tatooine for fuel and parts – an Outer Rim world, beyond the reach of the Trade Federation, where the Queen would be safe.

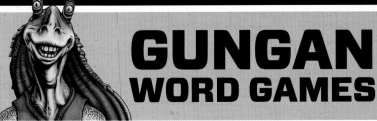

# GUNGAN
## WORD GAMES

The Gungans speak Gunganese – it's slightly similar to English. So, can you draw a line and match the Gunganese words to the English translation?

Duey

Ate-a

Mesa

Nutsen

Machineeks

Ex squeezee me

Mesa greeting, in peles mesa comen

Fraidee frog

Mesa doen nutten!

*I, I am, me, my*

*Droids or machines*

*Greetings, I come in peace.*

*I'm not doing anything!*

*Coward*

*Crazy*

*Eight*

*Two*

*Excuse me*

FACT FILE:
## Queen Amidala

**Name:** Padmé Naberrie of Naboo, Padmé Amidala, Queen Amidala of Naboo, Padmé Naberrie Skywalker
**Species:** Human
**Home planet:** Naboo
**Little known fact:** Padmé was crowned Queen at 14 years old, but was not the youngest Queen of Naboo ever to be elected
**Skills:** A brave and idealistic politician, determined to protect her people
**Weapon:** Royal blaster pistol

# NO TROUBLE FOR A SITH

The Viceroy tells Sidious that the Queen escaped Naboo and that they cannot track the ship – but it is no problem for Sidious' dark apprentice, Darth Maul. Can you draw the Sith's face watching from the darkness?

# THE ONLY HUMAN WHO COULD PODRACE . . .

The Queen's ship landed on the planet, Tatooine, and Qui-Gon, Jar Jar, R2-D2 and Padmé Amidala set out to buy the parts they needed for the ship. They went to a shop ran by a trader called Watto, who said that he had the parts but would not accept Qui-Gon's Republic credits to pay for them.

In the repair shop, they met Watto's slave, a boy called Anakin Skywalker. As Qui-Gon and the others were starting back to the ship, Anakin warned them that a storm was approaching and offered them shelter at home.

Over dinner, Anakin suggested a solution to Qui-Gon's problems – he could enter Anakin into the next day's podrace. The winnings would cover the cost of the parts they needed.

Observing Anakin's racing skills, Qui-Gon was amazed by his precision and intuition. "The Force is unusually strong with him," he said.

## "THERE IS SOMETHING ABOUT THIS BOY."
QUI-GON JINN

The next day, Qui-Gon made a bet with Watto that if Anakin lost the race he could have the starship. If Anakin won, Watto could keep the winnings and the podracer, but he would free Anakin and give them the parts they needed for their ship. Watto agreed.

Before the podrace began, Qui-Gon gave Ani some last minute advice. "Remember, concentrate on the moment. Feel, don't think. Use your instincts. May the Force be with you."

The racers blasted off! Anakin's devious rival Sebulba tried twice to sabotage him, but Ani's reflexes and skill at repairs saved him each time. By the final lap, the two were neck and neck in the lead.

On the final stretch, Sebulba began bashing into the side of Ani's podracer and they became entangled, side-by-side. As Sebulba tried to separate them, Ani pulled the thrusters and jetted off to the finishing line, leaving Sebulba to crash. Anakin had won!

Qui-Gon got the parts he needed for the ship and Anakin was free from slavery. Qui-Gon wanted to train him as a Jedi Knight!

# JEDI COUNCIL

When Anakin was tested by the Jedi Council, he had to say what was being shown on a screen that was turned away from him. Practise feeling the Force - look at this picture below for 20 seconds then cover it up.
Can you answer the questions from memory?

**1.** Can you see Master Yoda's feet?

No

**2.** What shape is Yoda's chair?

**3.** What colour is the sky?

Orange

**4.** What colour are the boots of the Jedi on the left?

orange

**5.** Three moons can be seen in the sky. True or false?

## "YOU MAY NOT TRAIN HIM."

The reason Yoda gives for not letting Qui-Gon begin training Anakin is written backwards and upside down below. Calm your mind to decipher what it says.

FUTURE IS. THIS BOYS CLOUDED

# JEDI VS SITH

**O**n Coruscant the Galactic Senate could not agree to help Queen Amidala, and in frustration she vowed to return home to Naboo to save her people. Darth Sidious, meanwhile, had sent his apprentice Darth Maul to assist the Trade Federation.

While the Queen's allies, the Gungans, faced the Trade Federation's battle droid army, the Queen, Qui-Gon, Obi-Wan and Anakin stormed the palace, intending to steal the aircraft they would need to attack the Federation battleship. They were confronted by Darth Maul, and as the Queen and the rest of the party escaped to the throne room, Qui-Gon and Obi-Wan drew their lightsabers and prepared to fight.

After a furious duel, Obi-Wan was trapped behind an energy shield, and could do nothing but watch as Maul got the better of Qui-Gon. The Sith stabbed Qui-Gon with his lightsaber, mortally wounding him.

**"I WILL FIND THEM QUICKLY, MASTER."**
**DARTH MAUL**

When the energy barrier opened, an angry Obi-Wan took on Darth Maul. Obi-Wan sliced Darth Maul's dual-lightsaber in half with his own, but the Sith apprentice used the Force to knock Obi-Wan into a pit. Obi-Wan had lost his own weapon, but thinking quickly, he saw Qui-Gon's lightsaber lying beside his wounded Master and, as he jumped up and out of the hole, used the Force to get the weapon. He took Maul by surprise and destroyed him with a single blow.

Obi-Wan ran to Qui-Gon's side.

"Obi-Wan, promise me you'll train the boy," a dying Qui-Gon told him. "He is the Chosen One. He will bring balance."

"Yes, Master," whispered Obi-Wan.

# THE RULE OF TWO

**Use the Force and spot the two images of Darth Maul that are the same.**

# MOVIE TRIVIA

**Do you think you know everything there is to know about *Star Wars*? Which of these Episode I film facts are true and which are false?**

1) Ewan McGregor (as Obi-Wan) made lightsaber noises as he duelled. These had to be edited out for the film.

☑ True   ■ False

2) Darth Maul has a total of fifteen horns on his head.

■ True   ■ False

3) To stop people copying the movie before it was shown in the cinema, the film was shipped under the name "The Doll House".

■ True   ■ False

4) Darth Maul never blinks during the film.

■ True   ■ False

5) The name Jar Jar was created by George Lucas.

■ True   ■ False

6) The word lightsaber is never used by any character during the film.

■ True   ■ False

# JEDI KNIGHTS:
## PROTECTORS OF THE PEACE

## THE JEDI CODE

*JEDI ARE THE GUARDIANS OF PEACE IN THE GALAXY.*

*JEDI USE THEIR POWERS TO DEFEND AND PROTECT, NEVER TO ATTACK OTHERS.*

*JEDI RESPECT ALL LIFE, IN ANY FORM.*

*JEDI SERVE OTHERS RATHER THAN RULING OVER THEM, FOR THE GOOD OF THE GALAXY.*

*JEDI SEEK TO IMPROVE THEMSELVES THROUGH KNOWLEDGE AND TRAINING.*

## JEDI COUNCIL

A Jedi Council was an organized body of Jedi, typically Masters, serving the Jedi Order as an administrative body that governed the Order's academies, temples, and organizations.

## GRAND MASTER

The Grand Master was the head of the Jedi Order. Yoda was the last Grand Master of the Old Republic before the Siths disbanded the Jedi Order.

## MASTER OF THE ORDER

The Master of the Order is the elected head of the Jedi Council. They had to be elected by unanimous vote from the High Council. Mace Windu was the last Master of the Order before the Jedi Purge.

## LIGHTSABERS

"TO USE A LIGHTSABER WELL WAS A MARK OF SOMEONE A CUT ABOVE THE ORDINARY." - OBI-WAN

The weapon consisted of a blade of pure plasma emitted from the hilt and suspended in a force containment field. To wield a lightsaber was to demonstrate incredible skill and confidence, as well as masterful dexterity and attunement to the Force.

**MACE WINDU**

**DARTH VADER**

**QUI-GON JINN**

**OBI-WAN KENOBI**

**WHAT COLOUR WOULD YOUR LIGHTSABER BE?**

## TOP FIVE JEDI FACTS

**1.** The Jedi are an ancient monastic order who are unified by their belief and observance of the Force.

**2.** Their official language is Galactic Basic Standard.

**3.** The official weapon of the Jedi is the lightsaber.

**4.** There are four ranks of Jedi: Jedi initiate, Jedi Padawan, Jedi Knight and Jedi Master.

**5.** As sanctioned peacekeepers of the galaxy, the Jedi were bound to find non-violent ways to resolve disputes between planets, but were occasionally required to use their superior martial-art skills to swiftly end unrest.

## JEDI ACADEMY

Jedi initiates, or Younglings, have to go through various trials before they are taken on as a Padawan for one-on-one training. An initiate would begin by spending a great deal of time in contemplation, learning to open himself up to the Force.

# CLONE ARMY

**A**fter several attempts had been made to assassinate Queen Amidala, the Supreme Chancellor and the Jedi Council assigned Obi-Wan and his Padawan, Anakin Skywalker, to protect her. They caught one suspected assassin, but before they could question her, an unknown bounty hunter shot her dead with a dart.

It was decided that for Padmé's safety she was to return to Naboo, with Anakin as her protector. Meanwhile, Obi-Wan traced the dart to an Outer Rim world called Kamino, the home of a race of cloners, and set out to find answers.

As he landed he was immediately greeted by a tall, elegant Kaminoan who said that the Prime Minister, Lama Su, was expecting him.

## "THE DARK SIDE CLOUDS EVERYTHING."
**MASTER YODA**

The Prime Minister told Obi-Wan that they were on schedule: two hundred thousand units were ready, with a million more on the way. Obi-Wan was instructed to tell the Master Sifo-Dyas that his order would be met on time.

"Master Sifo-Dyas was killed nearly ten years ago," said Obi-Wan.

"I'm sorry to hear that," replied Lama Su. "But I'm sure he would be proud of the army we've built for him. This army is for the Republic."

Obi-Wan was shown a huge clone army. The clones, Lama Su told him, could think creatively and were better than droids. They had been cloned from a bounty hunter called Jango Fett, whose genetic structure had been modified to make the clones more obedient. In return, Jango Fett asked for an unchanged clone for himself.

Obi-Wan discovered that Jango Fett had recently returned from a trip; Obi-Wan had found the bounty hunter he was looking for.

# WHO IS JANGO FETT?

**Jango Fett is hiding amongst his clones. Can you spot the real Jango? He's the only one who's different.**

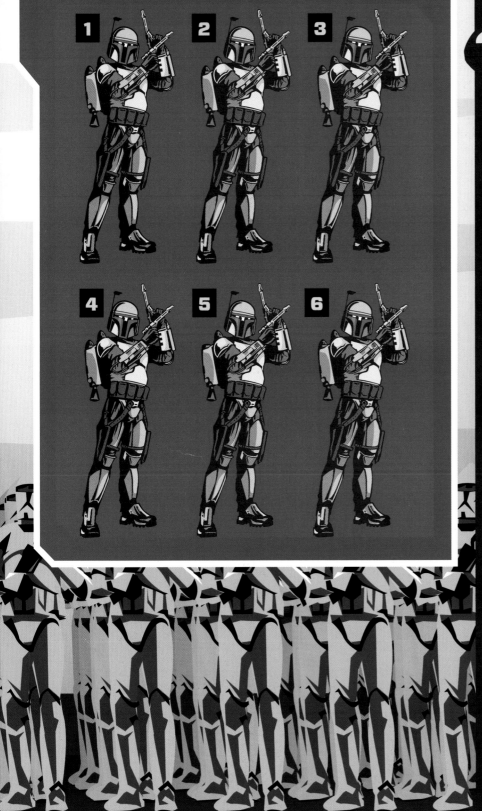

1
2
3
4
5
6

## CLONING: THE FACTS

**Confused about cloning? Never fear – here's all you need to know!**

- To make a clone, you first need a sample of someone's genetic code, or DNA. The Kaminoans used Jango Fett's DNA to make the clones.

- The donor cells would grow in artificial wombs which were filled with nutrients.

- The Kaminoans altered Jango's original DNA so the clones would be more obedient and easier to control as an army.

- The clones' growth was sped up so that a grown-up army wouldn't take a lifetime to produce.

- The clones would eventually become the feared Imperial stormtroopers.

- How quickly the clones would age was unknown – although it is thought to be twice the rate of natural-born humans.

# RESCUING OBI-WAN

**"ANI, I'M SO PROUD OF YOU."**
SHMI SKYWALKER

After spending days alone together on Naboo, Anakin expressed his true feelings for Padmé.

"From the moment I met you, all those years ago, not a day has gone by when I haven't thought about you," he said.

"You're studying to become a Jedi Knight. I'm a senator," said Padmé. "I will not let you give up your responsibilities, your future, for me."

That night, Anakin had a nightmare about his mother – she was suffering and in pain. He felt he had no choice but to go to his mother's rescue, and Padmé agreed to go with him.

When Anakin landed on Tatooine, Watto, his former slave master, told him that Shmi had married a man called Lars. Anakin and Padmé went to Lars' ranch and were greeted by the droid Anakin had built as a child, C-3PO. Anakin met Shmi's husband, who explained that Tusken Raiders had kidnapped her.

Anakin set off alone to rescue her. He found Shmi in a Tusken settlement, tied up and close to death.

"Ani, I'm so proud of you," said his mother, weakly. "I love you." With those words, she died.

Anakin, full of grief and anger, massacred the entire Tusken settlement.

Obi-Wan had fought the bounty hunter Jango Fett on Kaminoa, but Fett escaped. Obi-Wan chased him across the galaxy, and eventually tracked him to a planet called Geonosis. He saw lots of Federation ships and went to investigate. A giant automated factory was creating thousands of battle droids. He then heard voices and, following them, found a former Jedi, Count Dooku, discussing plans with the Viceroy of the Trade Federation. They plotted to join their armies together to overwhelm the Jedi, so that the Republic would agree to their demands.

Obi-Wan sent a message back to the Jedi Council, but was then attacked by a droideka and captured. The Master of the Jedi Council, Mace Windu, called for all available Jedi to go to Obi-Wan's rescue. He commanded that Anakin look after the senator, but Padmé agreed to go with Anakin to help Obi-Wan.

# ANAKIN'S PROMISE

Heartbroken from his mother's death, a devastated and angry Anakin makes a promise to Padmé. Use the code below to find out what it was.

| A | B | C | D | E | F | G | H | I | J | K | L | M | N | O | P | Q | R | S | T | U | V | W | X | Y | Z |
|---|---|---|---|---|---|---|---|---|---|---|---|---|---|---|---|---|---|---|---|---|---|---|---|---|---|
| 4 | 7 | 9 | 3 | 26 | 23 | 1 | 19 | 13 | 15 | 25 | 2 | 5 | 11 | 12 | 8 | 21 | 6 | 10 | 24 | 14 | 16 | 17 | 18 | 20 | 22 |

**13**       **17,13,2,2**       **7,26**       **24,19,26**       **5,12,10,24**

___       _____       ___       _____       _____

**8,12,17,26,6,23,14,2**       **15,26,3,13.**

_____       _____

# CHASING DOWN THE FETTS

Obi-Wan managed to attach a tracking device to Jango Fett's ship. Can you help Obi-Wan track him? Follow a path through the grid by moving across, up or down through the boxes that contain a number that can be divided by three.

**START**

| 33 | 30 | 3 | 25 | 25 | 0 | 35 | 5 | 35 | 25 | 35 | 5 | 35 | 8 | 8 |
|----|----|----|----|----|----|----|----|----|----|----|----|----|----|----|
| 35 | 35 | 9 | 10 | 10 | 20 | 20 | 20 | 22 | 24 | 11 | 19 | 20 | 24 | 20 |
| 20 | 25 | 12 | 15 | 18 | 25 | 25 | 25 | 25 | 25 | 25 | 25 | 25 | 25 | 25 |
| 20 | 25 | 22 | 23 | 6 | 0 | 35 | 5 | 35 | 25 | 35 | 13 | 11 | 10 | 11 |
| 10 | 1 | 11 | 10 | 9 | 20 | 20 | 20 | 22 | 24 | 11 | 13 | 24 | 22 | 1 |
| 1 | 10 | 1 | 1 | 12 | 25 | 25 | 25 | 25 | 25 | 25 | 2 | 2 | 2 | 2 |
| 2 | 4 | 8 | 8 | 3 | 10 | 7 | 13 | 11 | 10 | 11 | 22 | 7 | 14 | 7 |
| 25 | 25 | 25 | 25 | 9 | 14 | 14 | 13 | 24 | 22 | 1 | 14 | 14 | 14 | 14 |
| 35 | 25 | 35 | 13 | 18 | 33 | 30 | 2 | 2 | 2 | 2 | 32 | 32 | 32 | 32 |
| 22 | 24 | 11 | 13 | 32 | 32 | 18 | 22 | 22 | 21 | 33 | 30 | 22 | 22 | 22 |
| 22 | 22 | 25 | 25 | 25 | 25 | 21 | 3 | 6 | 9 | 22 | 21 | 26 | 26 | 26 |
| 26 | 26 | 35 | 25 | 35 | 13 | 26 | 26 | 26 | 26 | 26 | 18 | 15 | 12 | 21 |
| 29 | 29 | 22 | 24 | 11 | 13 | 29 | 29 | 29 | 29 | 29 | 29 | 29 | 29 | 24 |
| 0 | 35 | 5 | 35 | 25 | 35 | 26 | 35 | 25 | 35 | 13 | 23 | 23 | 24 | 9 |
| 20 | 20 | 20 | 22 | 24 | 11 | 29 | 22 | 24 | 11 | 13 | 7 | 5 | 8 | 3 |

**FINISH**

# THE ARENA

**C**ount Dooku entered the holding cell where Obi-Wan was restrained.

"Qui-Gon was once my apprentice, as you were his," Dooku told him. "He knew about the corruption in the Republic, but he would never have gone along with it if he knew the truth as I do. The Republic is now under the control of a Dark Lord called Darth Sidious."

"That's not possible. The Jedi would have sensed it," protested Obi-Wan.

"The dark side of the Force has clouded their vision. Join me, Obi-Wan and together we'll destroy the Sith."

"I'll never join you, Dooku," said Obi-Wan.

Padmé and Anakin arrived on Geonosis, but were ambushed and captured. As they were lead out into a gladiatorial stadium to die, Padmé told Anakin that she loved him too.

"I thought we had decided not to fall in love. That it would destroy our lives," said Anakin.

"I think our lives are about to be destroyed anyway," replied Padmé.

They were chained to tall poles in the centre

> ## "PATIENCE, VICEROY... SHE WILL DIE."
> COUNT DOOKU

of a giant arena, beside Obi-Wan, and ferocious beasts were let in to the arena to attack them. Padmé, Anakin and Obi-Wan all managed to free themselves. Anakin, using the Force, managed to tame one of the monsters, and the three of them got onto its back – but droidekas entered the stadium and surrounded them.

All seemed lost until Mace Windu appeared on the balcony where Count Dooku was watching.

"This party's over," said Windu. Around the stadium, lightsabers began to appear – the Jedi Knights were here.

Count Dooku smiled menacingly at Mace Windu. "Brave, my old Jedi friend, but foolish. You are hopelessly outnumbered."

The Jedi fought bravely, lightsabers against blasters and beasts. Mace Windu defeated the deadly Jango Fett, but before long the Jedi were overwhelmed by battle droids.

"It is finished – surrender!" called Dooku.

# A JEDI'S CHARACTER

Being a Jedi isn't an easy life – training and learning to be a Jedi and using the Force is a life-long process – even if you're 900 years old like Yoda! Can you circle all the words that describe a Jedi's character?

Training
Love Guidance
Focus
Impatience Loyalty Compassion Hate
Greed Faith Defence
Discipline Power Justice
Courage Anger
Perfection
Fear

FACT FILE:
Mace Windu

**Name:** Mace Windu
**Species:** Human
**Home planet:** Haruun Kal
**Little known fact:** Master Windu created Vaapad, the modern seventh form of lightsaber combat
**Skills:** Mace Windu is one of the Jedi Order's most formidable fighters, with his mastery of lightsaber combat and use of devastating Force powers in battle
**Weapon:** Lightsaber (purple)

# THE MASTER AND THE APPRENTICE

How much about the history of the Jedi and Sith do you know? Can you draw an arrow from each Master to their apprentice?

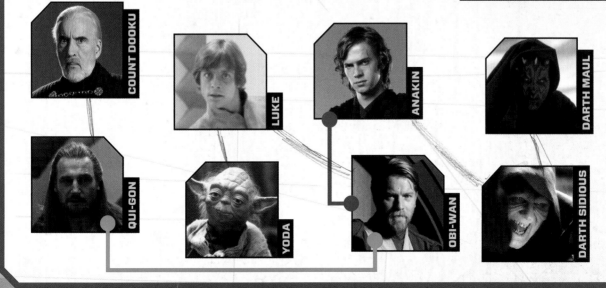

COUNT DOOKU

LUKE

ANAKIN

DARTH MAUL

QUI-GON

YODA

OBI-WAN

DARTH SIDIOUS

# THE BATTLE OF GEONOSIS

**S**uddenly, ships came down from the sky. It was Yoda with the Republic's new clone army. They formed a barrier around the survivors, who then all climbed aboard.

Obi-Wan and Anakin spotted Dooku flying away on a speeder. They followed Dooku to a hangar and chased him inside. Dooku stunned Anakin with Force lightning and then tried the same on Obi-Wan, who managed to absorb it with his lightsaber. A rapid duel followed.

Finally Dooku struck Obi-Wan on his arm and leg with his lightsaber and the noble Jedi fell to the ground. Dooku lifted his lightsaber to deliver the fatal blow, but Anakin jumped across and stopped Dooku's strike.

Anakin, with a lightsaber in each hand, fought Dooku, but was no match for the former Jedi Master. His right arm was severed at the elbow. But just as the triumphant Dooku turned to leave, Grand Master Yoda entered the hangar.

"The dark side I sense in you," said Yoda.

## "THE DARK SIDE I SENSE IN YOU."
### YODA

"I have become more powerful than any Jedi. Even you," he replied. "It is obvious that this contest can not be decided by our knowledge of the Force, but with our skills with a lightsaber."

"Fought well you have, my old Padawan," said Yoda as they locked lightsabers. At that moment, Dooku used the Force to fling a heavy metal pipe at the helpless Anakin and Obi-Wan. Yoda had no choice but to break off the duel and stop the pipe from crushing them; Dooku escaped.

Dooku returned to Coruscant where Darth Sidious was waiting for him.

"I have good news for you, Master," Count Dooku told his master. "The war has begun."

Despite galactic civil war, a recovered Anakin had more important plans. He escorted Padmé back to Naboo where, with R2-D2 and C-3PO as their witnesses, they were married.

# THE CLONE ARMY

Imagine that you had your own clone army. What sort of armour would your soldiers wear? What weapons would they have? Draw one below – make sure their armour protects them from the gunfire!

# DROID SEARCH

**The Clone Wars have begun and the battle droids are out in force. Can you find the following things amongst the troops?**

- ☐ A BATTLE DROID MISSING A RESTRAINING BOLT
- ☐ A BATTLE DROID MISSING AN ANTENNA
- ☐ A BATTLE DROID MISSING A HEAD
- ☐ A SUPER BATTLE DROID AIMING THE WRONG WAY
- ☐ A BATTLE DROID MISSING AN EYE
- ☐ A SUPER BATTLE DROID MISSING AN ARM

# DROID CLASS

**CLASS ONE:** Little more than computers, these droids are used to test medicines, make calculations, and help in the study of science and maths.

**CLASS TWO:** These droids were trained in engineering and were used on ships to make repairs, to explore new planets for natural resources, and to assist in the navigation of the ships.

**CLASS THREE:** These droids are programmed to interact with humans. They were often used in servitude, as child care and to interact with diplomats and royalty.

**CLASS FOUR:** These droids were fighters. They were used for security, as assassins, or in large armies. They were sometimes pitted against each other like gladiators for entertainment.

**CLASS FIVE:** These droids were used for menial labour. They were programmed to do the jobs that were too hazardous or to perform specialised tasks.

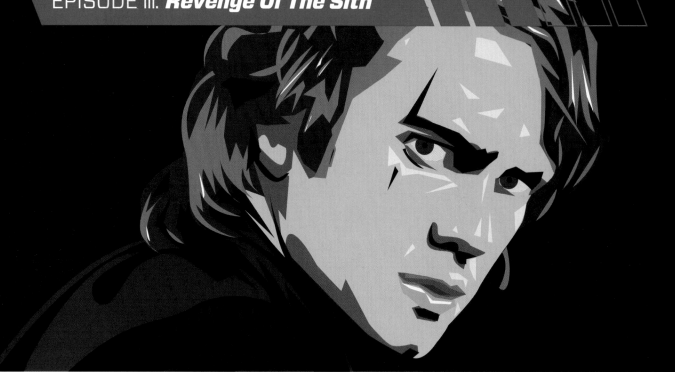

# TWICE THE PRIDE, DOUBLE THE FALL

**A**fter a fierce space battle, Obi-Wan and Anakin landed aboard the starship of General Grievous, the cyborg commander of Count Dooku's droid army. Grievous had captured the Republic's leader, Chancellor Palpatine, and the Jedi were on a rescue mission.

"I sense Count Dooku," Anakin told his master.

"I sense a trap," replied Obi-Wan.

Obi-Wan and Anakin found their way to where the Chancellor was being held, tied to a chair; sure enough, Count Dooku entered the room.

"Get help," said the Chancellor. "You're no match for him. He's a Sith Lord."

"Chancellor Palpatine, Sith Lords are our speciality," quipped Obi-Wan.

"My powers have doubled since we last met, Count," Anakin told him.

"Twice the pride, double the fall," said Dooku.

After a few blows, Dooku used the Force to choke Obi-Wan, then threw him to the other side of the room, where part of a balcony collapsed on top of him. Dooku continued to duel with Anakin, taunting him.

## "YOU WANTED REVENGE."
**CHANCELLOR PALPATINE**

"You have hate, you have anger, but you don't use them," Dooku told him. Suddenly, Anakin saw an opening and sliced off both Dooku's hands with his lightsaber. Anakin caught Dooku's weapon and placed both lightsabers either side of Dooku's neck.

"Good, Anakin, good," laughed the Chancellor. "I knew you could do it. Kill him. Kill him now!"

Reluctantly, Anakin uncrossed the lightsabers taking off Count Dooku's head.

"I shouldn't have done that. It's not the Jedi way," said Anakin. "I couldn't stop myself."

"It is only natural. He cut off your arm. You wanted revenge." replied the Chancellor. "It wasn't the first time, Anakin. Remember what you told me about your mother and the Sand People."

They made a quick escape, Anakin carrying the unconscious Obi-Wan on his back, and made it back to Coruscant – but since General Grievous had escaped, the Clone Wars would continue.

# GALACTIC
## WORDSEARCH

How many *Star Wars* character names can you find in the wordsearch below? You're going to have to use the Force to find them on your own, as they're not listed . . .

| B | S | A | M | T | C | W | E | L | S |
|---|---|---|---|---|---|---|---|---|---|
| U | G | A | I | L | P | S | N | Z | U |
| C | C | N | P | E | W | N | I | C | R |
| Q | M | A | M | Z | L | O | T | I | M |
| X | L | K | O | B | I | W | A | N | D |
| Y | W | I | S | D | I | U | P | F | B |
| V | O | N | L | N | C | A | L | J | F |
| A | K | A | D | M | A | F | A | U | S |
| A | A | U | M | K | X | T | P | U | S |
| B | C | C | K | I | T | H | O | J | G |
| G | Z | C | A | Z | D | V | Q | J | R |
| Y | K | G | A | B | E | A | B | U | I |
| C | E | T | U | B | W | Q | L | N | E |
| K | C | D | R | J | W | E | F | A | V |
| S | Q | G | J | Y | P | E | H | M | O |
| O | P | D | J | B | X | V | H | A | U |
| A | D | O | Y | J | C | R | P | C | S |
| D | A | M | I | D | A | L | A | Q | J |
| O | G | D | T | I | R | E | X | P | O |
| H | N | Z | A | Q | R | G | G | V | P |

OK, here's a hint: there are 9 names to find.

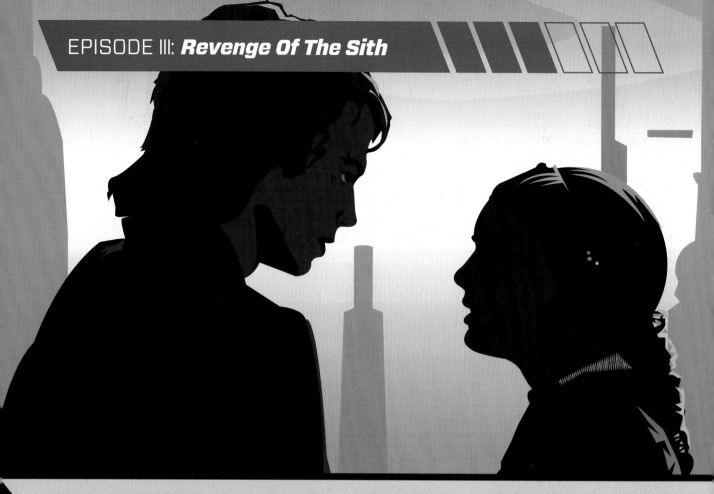

# DARTH PLAGUEIS

**A**s soon as they landed, Anakin was taken to see the senators, who thanked him for his bravery in rescuing the Chancellor.

"Something wonderful has happened. Ani, I'm pregnant," Padmé told him, when he saw her.

Anakin was overjoyed, but that night he had a nightmare about Padmé dying in childbirth. He made a vow that this would never come true.

The next day, Chancellor Palpatine told Anakin that he had been granted emergency powers from the senate, giving him control over the Jedi Order. He appointed Anakin as his personal representative on the Jedi Council. Begrudingly, the Council accepted Anakin's appointment, but would not yet grant him the rank of Jedi Master.

After the Council session, Obi-Wan told Anakin that the Council would like Anakin to report on all the Chancellor's dealings – to spy on him for the Jedi Order.

"The Chancellor is not a bad man, Obi-Wan. He befriended me. He's watched out for me ever since I arrived here," said Anakin. "You're asking me to do something against the Jedi code, against a mentor and a friend."

## "THEY'RE PLANNING TO BETRAY ME."
**CHANCELLOR PALPATINE**

Later, Palpatine asked Anakin if he had ever heard the tragedy of Darth Plagueis the Wise.

"It's not a story the Jedi would tell you. It's a Sith legend. Darth Plagueis was a dark lord so powerful, and so wise, that he could even keep the ones he cared about from dying."

"He could actually save people from death?" asked Anakin.

"The dark side of the Force is a pathway to many abilities some consider to be unnatural."

"Is it possible to learn this power?" asked Anakin, eagerly.

"Not from a Jedi," replied Palpatine.

Anakin, confused and losing trust in the Jedi Order, spoke to Padmé.

"Something's wrong. I'm not the Jedi I should be," he said. "I want more and I know I shouldn't."

"I'm worried about you. You expect too much of yourself," said Padmé.

"I've found a way to save you from my nightmare. I won't lose you, Padmé."

# GET GRIEVOUS!

Obi-Wan sets off to confront General Grievous. Can you help him find his way though the maze to find the droid leader?

**START**

**FINISH**

# CODE: VICTORY

**When Obi-Wan finally defeats Grievous, he shoots him in the chest with a blaster gun.**

What does he say about blaster guns? Each letter has been shifted two letters further in the alphabet – can you decode what he says?

## W P E K X K N K U G F

# THE DARK SIDE

**A**nakin went to see the Chancellor. "How do you know the ways of the Force?" asked Anakin.

"My mentor taught me all about the ways of the Force. Even the nature of the dark side. Only through me will you be able to save your wife from certain death," Palpatine said.

Anakin realised that Palpatine was the Sith Lord, Dooku's master. He drew his lightsaber.

"Are you going to kill me?" Palaptine asked.

"I'd certainly like to," said Anakin, but he withdrew his lightsaber. "I'm going to turn you over to the Jedi Council."

Quickly, Anakin told Mace Windu all he knew about Palpatine. Anakin offered his help in arresting the Chancellor, but Windu, sensing confusion and fear in him, sent Anakin to the Council chambers. Windu went to the Chancellor's quarters with a guard of Jedi.

"You're under arrest, Chancellor. The Senate will decide your fate," said Windu.

"I am the Senate," Palpatine snarled, drawing

**"I TOLD YOU IT WOULD COME TO THIS."**
— CHANCELLOR PALPATINE

his lightsaber. He quickly destroyed all the Jedi Knights, leaving only him and Windu.

Anakin had disobeyed Windu's orders and ran to the Chancellor's quarters. When Anakin arrived, he found the Chancellor lying on the floor with Windu standing over him.

"The Jedi are taking over," called the Chancellor, desparately, shooting Force Lightning at Windu. Windu absorbed it using his lightsaber, and using this power quickly took its toll on the Chancellor's strength.

"I have the power to save the one you love. You must choose," the Chancellor told Anakin.

"I am going to end this once and for all," said Windu. "He's too dangerous to be left alive."

"Please, I need him," shouted Anakin and, using his lightsaber, cut off Windu's arm. The Chancellor smiled and used his lightning to fling the wounded Jedi out of the open window.

# CHARACTER ANAGRAMS

The dark side has clouded the Force and the names of these famous Jedi have been scrambled. Can you use your powers to put them back in the right order?

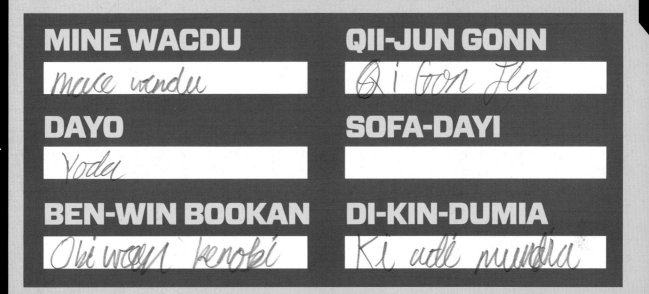

**MINE WACDU**

*mace wndu*

**DAYO**

*Yoda*

**BEN-WIN BOOKAN**

*Obi wan kenobi*

**QII-JUN GONN**

*Qi Gon Jin*

**SOFA-DAYI**

**DI-KIN-DUMIA**

*Ki adi mundi*

# THE BIRTH OF DARTH VADER

When Anakin turns to the dark side, he is given a new Sith name, Darth Vader. Only one of the sentences below is true . . . which is it?

1) Anakin agrees to turn to the dark side, if the Chancellor will help Anakin save Padmé's life.

2) Anakin agrees to turn to the dark side, if he can kill Obi-Wan himself.

3) The Chancellor uses mind tricks to convince Anakin to join the dark side.

4) Anakin turns to the dark side, but he doesn't think he needs the Chancellor to learn how to cheat death.

# ORDER 66

**P**alpatine declared himself Emperor and commanded Anakin – Darth Vader – to kill all the Jedi in the Jedi Temple. "Show no mercy. Only then will you be strong enough with the dark side to save Padmé," he said.

He then initiated 'Order 66'. This was the order to the clone army to kill all the Jedi – but Obi-Wan and Yoda both managed to escape. On Coruscant, Obi-Wan checked the security footage and discovered Anakin's betrayal.

To find Anakin, Obi-Wan hid aboard Padmé's ship when she went to find her husband. When Padmé arrived, Vader believed that she had betrayed him by leading Obi-Wan to him, so he choked his wife with the Force.

"You've turned her against me," Vader shouted at Obi-Wan.

"Your anger and your lust for power have already done that," said Obi-Wan, sadly.

"If you're not with me, then you're my enemy." snarled Vader, attacking with fury.

The duel began, as the former Master and Padawan fought a long battle on floating platforms above a river of molten lava.

Meanwhile, on Coruscant, Yoda confronted Darth Sidious in the Senate chamber, where the

## "ONLY A SITH DEALS IN ABSOLUTES."
**OBI-WAN KENOBI**

Emperor used all the power of the dark side to cast Yoda down. The Grand Master fell to the bottom of the Senate chamber and retreated.

"It's over, Anakin. I have the higher ground," Obi-Wan shouted, as their duel continued.

"You underestimate my power," called Vader as he jumped into the air towards Obi-Wan. With one swift movement, Obi-Wan chopped off both Vader's legs and arm, leaving him just above the lava river.

"You were the Chosen One! You were supposed to bring balance to the Force, not leave it in darkness," cried a tearful Obi-Wan, as he picked up Vader's lightsaber.

Vader, still alive, was later picked up by the Emperor. He was taken back to Coruscant and fitted into a life-support suit.

Vader asked the Chancellor, in his new electronic voice, "Where is Padmé?"

"It seems, in your anger, you killed her," the Emperor lied.

Distraught, Vader broke free from the operating table and cried out in anguish.

# DEATH STAR
## THE ULTIMATE WEAPON

**"THIS IS A MACHINE OF WAR SUCH AS THE UNIVERSE HAS NEVER KNOWN."**

**Name:** Death Star
**Conceived by:** Raith Sienar
**Designed by:** Imperial Department of Miltary Research
**Affiliation:** Galactic Empire

**Size:** As big as a small moon
**Purpose:** To destroy rebel planets and create fear within the Empire

The Death Star was a giant Imperial battle station with a built-in superlaser that could destroy planets.

**Cell block 1138** – Han and Luke dress up as stormtroopers in order to go undetected when they attempt to rescue Leia. They pretend Chewie is their prisoner so they can enter the detention area aboard the Death Star.

**Trash compactor** – Luke, Han, and Chewie infiltrate the Death Star to free Princess Leia. While making their escape, they dive down a garbage chute and become trapped in a trash compactor with a hungry dianoga. Then the walls begin to close in on them, and our heroes are caught in a tight squeeze!

**Hangar Bay 327** – While the rebel forces disable the tractor beam in the Death Star's main docking area, Master and apprentice meet once more. Darth Vader and Obi-Wan duel to the death.

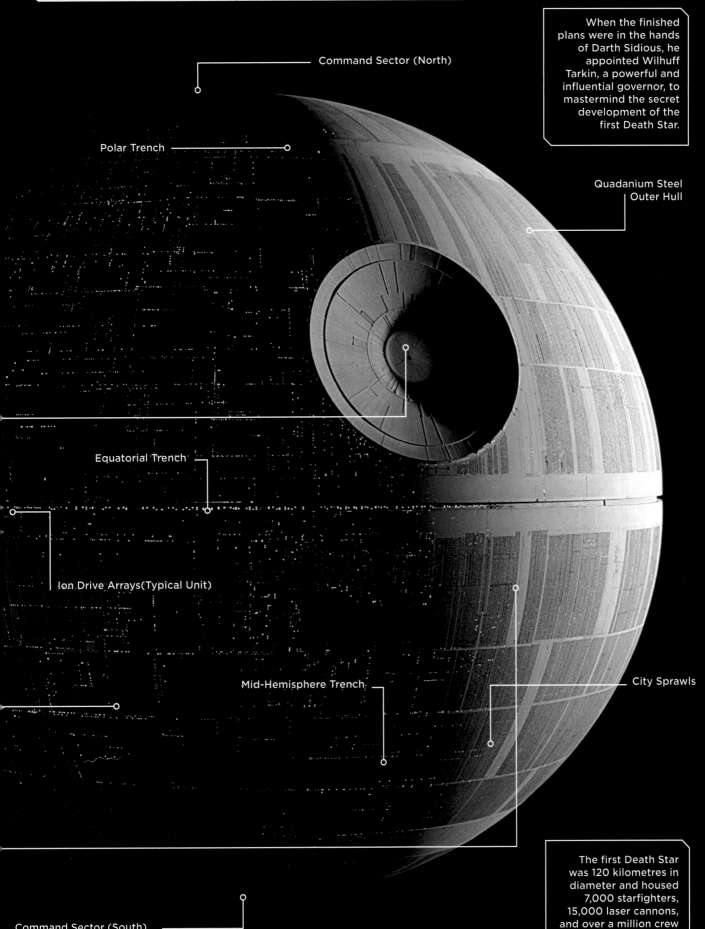

Command Sector (North)

Polar Trench

When the finished plans were in the hands of Darth Sidious, he appointed Wilhuff Tarkin, a powerful and influential governor, to mastermind the secret development of the first Death Star.

Quadanium Steel Outer Hull

Equatorial Trench

Ion Drive Arrays(Typical Unit)

Mid-Hemisphere Trench

City Sprawls

Command Sector (South)

The first Death Star was 120 kilometres in diameter and housed 7,000 starfighters, 15,000 laser cannons, and over a million crew members and troops

# THE JEDI PATH

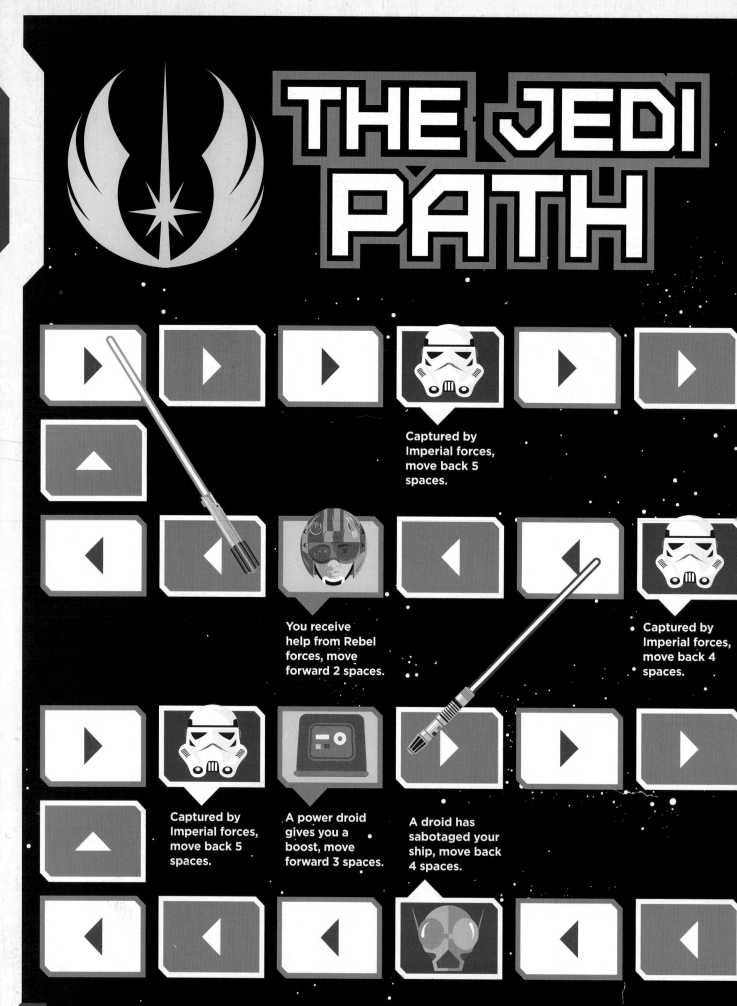

Captured by Imperial forces, move back 5 spaces.

You receive help from Rebel forces, move forward 2 spaces.

Captured by Imperial forces, move back 4 spaces.

Captured by Imperial forces, move back 5 spaces.

A power droid gives you a boost, move forward 3 spaces.

A droid has sabotaged your ship, move back 4 spaces.

**You will need:**
- 2-6 players
- Something to act as counters (e.g. coins, buttons)
- A die
- The Force

**How to play:**
Take turns to roll the die and move around the board. If you land on a space with a lightsaber, move forward to the space that it points to. If you land on a space with a character, then follow the instructions. Remember, Luke will help you but the stormtroopers will knock you back.

First to the finish is the ultimate Jedi Master!

You are a Jedi Master!

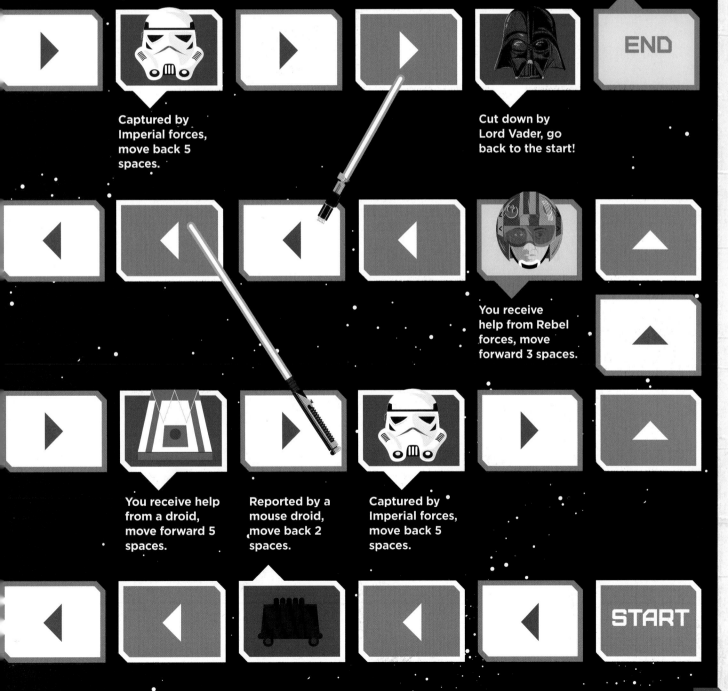

**END**

Captured by Imperial forces, move back 5 spaces.

Cut down by Lord Vader, go back to the start!

You receive help from Rebel forces, move forward 3 spaces.

You receive help from a droid, move forward 5 spaces.

Reported by a mouse droid, move back 2 spaces.

Captured by Imperial forces, move back 5 spaces.

**START**

# A BOY ON TATOOINE

**P**rincess Leia's ship was attacked by Imperial forces. A fiery battle raged as stormtroopers boarded. A large figure, cloaked in black, swept through the carnage.

As C-3PO ran around in panic, he spotted R2-D2 with Princess Leia. Leia ran to escape, but was stunned by a stormtrooper. R2-D2 and C-3PO got in to an escape pod and launched.

The droids crashed in a desert. R2-D2 told C-3PO that he was on a mission – but they were soon captured by Jawa traders. Meanwhile, stormtroopers had followed the droids' escape pod and were searching the desert.

R2-D2 and C-3PO were marched out of the transporter vessel to be sold to a local farmer. A boy called Luke Skywalker and his uncle, Owen Lars, were looking to buy a translator droid. C-3PO told Owen that he was fluent in many languages so he was hired. Since the R2

### "HELP ME, OBI-WAN KENOBI."
**PRINCESS LEIA**

unit Owen had first chosen blew up, C-3PO convinced Luke that his friend, R2-D2, was more than reliable and so both the droids followed Luke back to the farm.

Later, as Luke serviced his two new droids, he triggered something inside R2-D2. An image of Princess Leia was projected and part of a message began to play in a loop: "Help me, Obi-Wan Kenobi. You're my only hope."

Luke said that he knew an old Ben Kenobi who lived in the caves near the farm and that they must be related. R2-D2 refused to play the message to anyone but Obi-Wan.

When Luke returned back to his room after dinner, he discovered that R2-D2 had run away to find Obi-Wan alone...

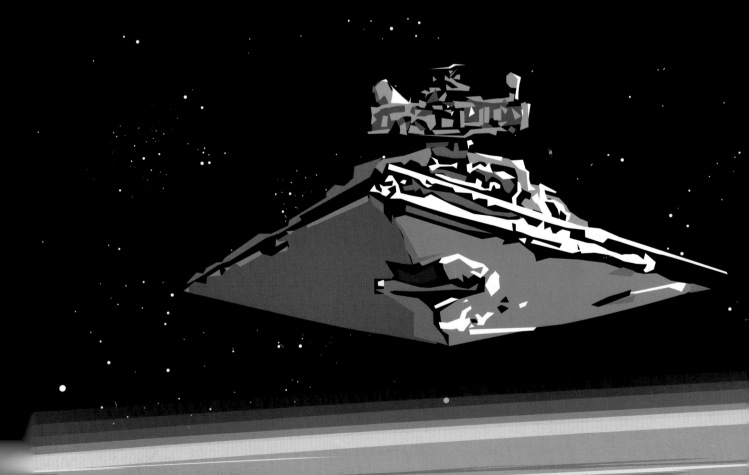

# CHARACTER CLOSE-UPS

## How well do you think you know the characters from *Star Wars*?

Can you recognise these characters from their close-ups?

**1**
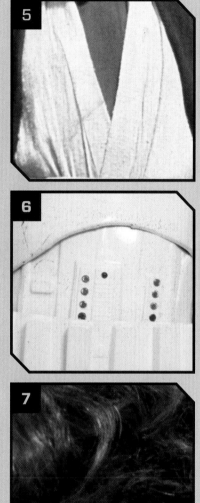

**5**

**2**
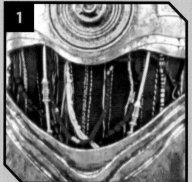

**6**

**3**

**7**
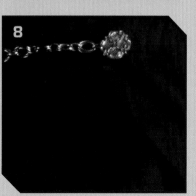

**4**
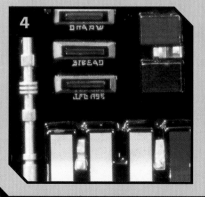

**8**

# LUKE AND OBI-WAN

**E**arly the next morning, Luke and C-3PO went in search of R2-D2. They soon found him, but were attacked by the Sand People and Luke was knocked unconscious. A cloaked figure scared the Sand People away. Luke awoke to see it was Ben Kenobi, and told him of R2-D2's search for his former master, Obi-Wan.

"Now, that's a name I haven't heard for a long time," replied Ben. "He's me."

Obi-Wan said that Luke's father had been a Jedi Knight who fought in the Clone Wars, along with Obi-Wan himself.

"Your father wanted you to have this, when you were old enough," he said, as he dug something out of an old chest. It was Luke's father's lightsaber – the weapon of a Jedi Knight.

Luke asked Obi-Wan how his father had died. "A young Jedi called Darth Vader, who was a pupil of mine until he turned to the dark side of the Force, betrayed and murdered your father," Obi-Wan told him.

R2-D2 played Princess Leia's message:

"General Kenobi, years ago you served my father in the Clone Wars. Now he begs you to help him in his struggle against the Empire. I have placed information vital to the survival of

the rebellion into the memory systems of this R2 unit. You must see this droid safely delivered to him on Alderaan."

Obi-Wan told Luke that he must learn the ways of the Force and go with him to Alderaan. Luke was not convinced, but he did agree to give Obi-Wan a lift to wherever he needed to go. On the way Luke and Obi-Wan found the Jawa transporter destroyed by stormtroopers. They had been trying to track down the droids.

Luke raced home, only to find that stormtroopers had got there first and the farm was in cinders.

There was nothing left for Luke on Tatooine now, so he went with Obi-Wan.

Meanwhile, on the Death Star, the Empire were planning their next move to destroy the Rebel Alliance. To scare Princess Leia into telling them the location of the hidden rebel base, Grand Moff Tarkin had given the order to destroy Alderaan, Leia's home planet. In desperation, Leia told the General what he wanted to know – but he still destroyed Alderaan with a single blast.

> "BOY, AM I GLAD TO SEE YOU!"
> LUKE SKYWALKER

# OBI-WAN SUDOKU

**Can you fill the missing letters in the grid below so there's only one of each of the letters in Obi-Wan's name in each row and column?**

|   | N |   |   | I |   |
|---|---|---|---|---|---|
| I | O | W |   | B |   |
|   |   | A | O | W | I |
| O | W | I | B |   |   |
|   | I |   | A | N | B |
|   | N |   | I |   |   |

**Name:** Obi-Wan Kenobi, Ben Kenobi
**Species:** Human
**Home planet:** Stewjon
**Little known fact:** 'Old Ben' the hermit is actually one of the last surviving Jedi Knights, a veteran of the Clone Wars
**Skills:** Obi-Wan is no longer as great a swordsman as he once was, but his mastery of the Force is greater than ever
**Weapon:** Lightsaber (blue)

# FORCE POWERS

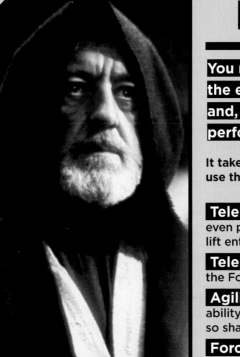

**You must learn the ways of the Force! The Force is the energy field that binds all living things together, and, when harnessed, allows Jedi and Sith Masters to perform superhuman feats.**

It takes many years to develop the control and wisdom required to use the Force. Patience, young Padawan!

**Telekinesis:** Use the Force to push, pull and pick up objects and even people without touching them. Master Yoda has been known to lift entire spacecraft.

**Telepathy:** Jedi can sense each other and communicate using the Force, even across vast distances.

**Agility:** Force users are capable of astonishing speed, jumping ability, and can even defy gravity for short periods. Their reflexes are so sharp they can even deflect blaster bolts with their lightsabers.

**Force Lightning:** A frightening ability developed by the Dark Lords of the Sith, Force Lightning lets the Force user shoot deadly bolts of electricity from their fingertips.

# "YOUR POWERS ARE WEAK, OLD MAN."

**"THAT'S NO MOON."**
OBI-WAN KENOBI

Luke and Obi-Wan recruited Han Solo and his co-captain, Chewbacca, to fly them to Alderaan on their spaceship, the *Millennium Falcon*. When they arrived at Alderaan, all they found was an asteroid field ... and the Death Star. Han and Chewie tried to turn the *Falcon* back, but it was too late. They were caught in the tractor beam and pulled on board.

Darth Vader and the stormtroopers boarded the *Millennium Falcon* – but found no one. When the coast was clear, Han, Luke, Obi-Wan and Chewie emerged from smuggling compartments.

Han and Luke set off to rescue Princess Leia. With the droids' help they found the way to the detention centre and broke Leia out of her cell.

Meanwhile, Obi-Wan located the main power generator for the tractor beam and shut it down. But Darth Vader had sensed Obi-Wan's presence on board and come to face his old enemy.

"I've been waiting for you, Obi-Wan. We meet again at last," said Vader. "The circle is now complete. When I last saw you I was but a learner. Now I am the master."

"Only a master of evil, Darth," said Obi-Wan as they began to fight. "You can't win. If you strike me down I shall become more powerful than you can possibly imagine."

Luke, Leia and Han fought their way back to the ship. Luke saw Obi-Wan fighting Vader. He turned, smiled at Luke and stepped back, holding his lightsaber in front of his face. Darth Vader swung and struck Obi-Wan, who vanished, leaving his cloak in a pile on the floor.

Luke screamed in shock, which alerted the stormtroopers; Luke, Han, Leia, Chewie, R2-D2 and C-3PO boarded the *Millennium Falcon*, took off and escaped from the Death Star.

# HOW TO DRAW DARTH VADER

He was the Chosen One and a terrifying Sith Lord. Can you draw Darth Vader? Let's find out!

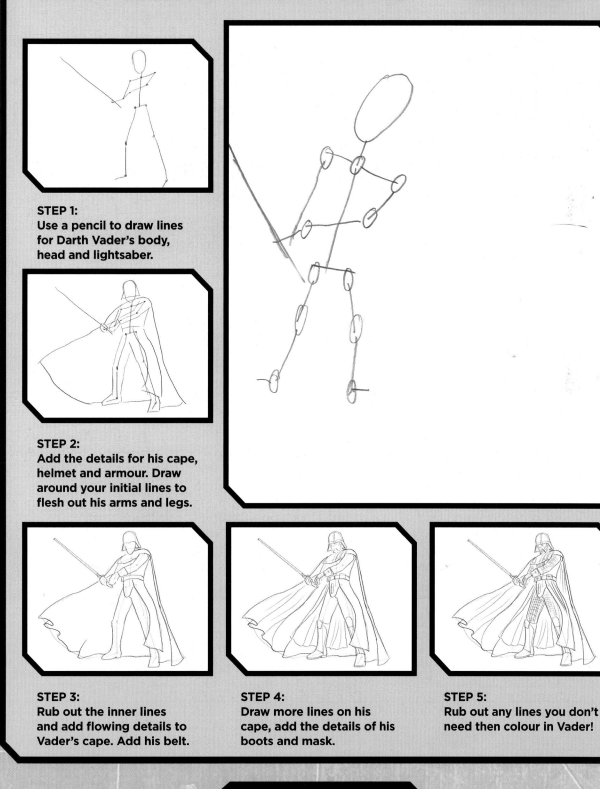

**STEP 1:**
Use a pencil to draw lines for Darth Vader's body, head and lightsaber.

**STEP 2:**
Add the details for his cape, helmet and armour. Draw around your initial lines to flesh out his arms and legs.

**STEP 3:**
Rub out the inner lines and add flowing details to Vader's cape. Add his belt.

**STEP 4:**
Draw more lines on his cape, add the details of his boots and mask.

**STEP 5:**
Rub out any lines you don't need then colour in Vader!

# DESTRUCTION OF THE DEATH STAR

**A**s the *Millennium Falcon* landed at the Rebel base on a moon of the planet Yavin, Leia handed over R2-D2 to the Rebel commander. Using the secret blueprints they planned a mission to destroy the station.

The weakness of the Death Star was a small exhaust vent. A one-man fighter craft would have to approach down through a trench on the surface and shoot a torpedo into the vent. A precise hit would start off a chain reaction and would explode the main reactor.

Luke was ready to climb aboard his ship to join the attack, but Han had received his reward for the rescue of Leia and was leaving. Luke tried to get him to join the fight, but Han still refused. With R2 at his side, Luke climbed into his ship.

Red Squadron, in their X-wing fighters, started their attack. Some of the fighters drew fire from the Death Star, while others took it in turns to fly down the trench to try and hit the exhaust

> ## "THE FORCE IS STRONG IN THIS ONE."
> — **DARTH VADER**

vent. Luke's first attempt at the trench run was blocked by heavy fire from an Imperial ship.

The Rebels were getting too close, so Darth Vader decided to end this attack himself. After several failed attempts at firing a blast into the exhaust vent, it was Luke's turn again. Just as Luke was about to set his targeting computer, he heard Obi-Wan's voice again telling him to use the Force instead. Darth Vader locked his guns onto Luke's ship, but was suddenly fired at from above – it was Han in the *Millennium Falcon*! This gave Luke time to make the shot. He turned off his computers and fired his blaster ... it was a hit! The Death Star exploded and was destroyed.

At a big ceremony, Princess Leia rewarded Luke, Han and Chewie with medals for their heroism.

# DEATH STAR MAZE

Luke and the Rebels need to destroy the Death Star. Using the Force, can you guide Luke's blast through the maze into the exhaust port to blow up the station's main reactor?

# MILLENNIUM FALCON

## THE FASTEST HUNK OF JUNK IN THE GALAXY

### "MODIFIED. HEAVILY MODIFIED. ILLEGALLY MODIFIED."

Escape Pods

Cockpit

**Name:** *Millennium Falcon*
**Manufacturer:** Corellian Engineering Corporation
**Model:** YT-1300f light freighter
**Owner and pilot:** Han Solo
**Co-pilot:** Chewbacca
**Length:** 34 meters
**Width:** 25 meters
**Notable equipment:** Avatar-10 hyperdrive, navigational deflector system, duralloy plating, stellar navigation sensors, Rubicon navigation computer
**Weapons:** Quad-laser cannons, concussion missile tubes, surface defense blaster cannon

The *Falcon* comes to Luke's rescue as he attempts to blow up the Death Star. Han swoops in and takes out a TIE fighter hot on the heels of the brave new Jedi.

The ship was incredibly fast, capable of attaining 0.5 past lightspeed and could make the Kessel Run (an infamous smugglers' route that should take 18 parsecs) in less than 12 parsecs.

The Rebels are on a mission to destroy the second Death Star. Han relinquishes control of the *Falcon* to Lando and his co-pilot, Nien Nunb. The two rebels fly to the core of the Death Star and successfully destroy it.

The *Falcon* underwent many modifications from all its many owners. It was used for different purposes; as a hospital, a smuggler's freighter, in battle, and therefore needed different technology to fulfil its different roles. Also, after many collisions and attacks, there were endless repairs to be made. When the *Falcon* was last seen in 44 ABY, it was virtually unrecognisable as the ship that was commissioned in 60 BBY.

## FACT FILE:
## Han Solo

**Name:** Han Solo
**Species:** Human
**Home planet:** Corellia
**Little known fact:** Han won the *Millennium Falcon* from Lando Calrissian in a game of sabacc
**Skills:** Besides his well-known skill as a starship pilot, Han is notoriously quick on the draw
**Weapon:** Heavy blaster pistol

Quad Laser Canon

Sensor Dish

Forward Mandibles

Deflector Shield Projector

## FACT FILE:
## Chewie

**Name:** Chewbacca
**Species:** Wookiee
**Home planet:** Kashyyyk
**Little known fact:** Chewie has claws, but it is dishonourable to use them for fighting – they are strictly for climbing
**Skills:** A brilliant engineer, Chewbacca made many of the *Falcon*'s modifications
**Weapon:** Bowcaster

The *Millennium Falcon* was a freight ship with a colourful past. Han Solo won the *Falcon* in a bet over a game of sabacc with Lando Calrissian. Han and his Wookiee co-pilot, Chewie, were smugglers, and made good use of the ships many hiding places for storing their cargo.

# BATTLE OF HOTH

**C**ommander Luke Skywalker was patrolling the area surrounding Echo Base on the planet Hoth when a wampa knocked him to the ground. Back at the base, Han Solo was concerned that Luke had not returned. With the temperatures dropping rapidly, Han saddled a tauntaun and set off to rescue his friend.

Meanwhile, Luke found himself hanging upside down in the wampa's cave. He used the Force to catch his lightsaber, cut himself down and chop off the angry wampa's arm before escaping.

Han finally found Luke unconscious in the snow. He used Luke's lightsaber to cut open the tauntaun, keeping Luke warm inside while Han built a shelter. As Luke slept, Obi-Wan's spirit appeared to him, telling him to seek Master Yoda on the planet Dagobah and complete his training. In the morning, the pair were rescued.

Later, the Rebel sensors detected an Imperial probe droid. With their base on the verge of

> ## "IT ISN'T FRIENDLY, WHATEVER IT IS."
> — HAN SOLO

being discovered, the Rebels prepared for battle.

The Empire's AT-AT walkers were approaching the base, firing lasers at the base's power gererators. Blaster fire just bounced off their thick armour. Luke thought of a new strategy. "Use your harpoons and tow cables!" A Rebel snowspeeder looped a cable around a walker's legs and it collapsed to the ground.

The assault on Echo Base was too heavy for the Rebel forces. As stormtroopers entered the base, Princess Leia called for evacuation.

Out on the battlefield, Luke's snowspeeder had been destroyed, but he still managed to destroy an AT-AT using his lightsaber.

Luke ran back to the base on foot, where R2-D2 was waiting for him in the ship. They took off quickly, leaving the Battle of Hoth behind.

# WALKER WORK OF ART

Use the grid to help you copy this picture of an Imperial AT-AT.

# CREATURES OF HOTH

## WAMPA

Hoth's most feared predators, wampas can grow up to three metres tall and weigh up to 200 kilograms. Their razor-sharp claws let them dig lairs out of the ice.

## TAUNTAUN

Tauntauns are warm-blooded herd creatures used by the Rebels on Hoth as pack beasts and riding animals. They are the main prey of the planet's wampas.

# THE WAY OF THE FORCE

**A**s Luke and R2 descended into the thick, foggy atmosphere of Dagobah, all the scopes on the ship died and Luke couldn't see anything! He tried to land, but crashed into a murky swamp. As the X-wing sank, Luke and R2-D2 started their search for Yoda.

They ran into a small green alien with large pointy ears and a walking-stick. He told them that he knew where they could find the Jedi Master Yoda, but Luke's frustration got the better of him. "This is a waste of time!" he yelled.

"I cannot teach him. The boy has no patience," the green alien said to the air.

"He will learn patience," replied the voice of Obi-Wan.

"Hmm. Much anger in him, like his father. He is not ready," said the green alien – who Luke now realised was Master Yoda himself.

"Yoda? I won't fail. I'm not afraid," Luke said.

"You will be," Yoda replied.

Luke's Jedi training began immediately.

> **"THIS IS A WASTE OF TIME."**
> — LUKE SKYWALKER

Yoda had Luke running through the swamps of Dagobah, climbing up long vines and swinging through the trees, all with Yoda on his back.

"The Jedi's strength flows from the Force," taught Yoda. "But beware of the dark side. Anger, fear, aggression - the dark side of the force are they. Consume you it will, like it did Obi-Wan's apprentice."

"Vader," finished Luke. "But how will I know the good side from the bad?"

"You will know," promised Yoda.

Meanwhile, on the Death Star, the Emperor told Darth Vader how valuable the son of Anakin Skywalker could be to the Empire's cause.

"He could destroy us," said Palpatine.

Vader promised that he could turn Luke to the dark side. "He will join us or die, my Master."

# ARE YOU AS WISE AS YODA?

## Answer these questions to find out.

**1) Which of these is the home planet of the Wookiee?**

**A.** Kashyyyk
**B.** Tatooine
**C.** Wookieen

**2) Which ship made the Kessel Run in less than 12 parsecs?**

**A.** TIE fighter
**B.** *Millennium Falcon*
**C.** X-wing fighter

**3) What does AT-AT stand for?**

**A.** All Terror All Terrain
**B.** Automatic Team Attack Tanks
**C.** All Terrain Armoured Transport

FACT FILE:
**Yoda**

**Name:** Yoda
**Species:** Unknown
**Home planet:** Unknown
**Little known facts:** Though he is many hundreds of years old, and only 0.66 metres tall, Yoda is perhaps the Galaxy's most powerful Jedi Master
**Skills:** Great wisdom, and mastery of Force powers and lightsaber combat rivalled only by the Dark Lord of the Sith, Darth Sidious
**Weapon:** Lightsaber (green), concealed in his cane

# JEDI TRAINING

**So you think you have what it takes to be a Jedi? Here are some simple tips so you can be at one with the force.**

**You will need:**
• a tennis ball
• a friend (or a wall)

Throwing and catching is a great way to improve your hand-eye co-ordination and keep those Jedi reflexes sharp! Practise catching the ball with both hands first, then catch with just one hand, alternating between your left and right hands.
**Is the Force strong with you?** Try using more than one ball.
**Are you a Jedi Master?** Write a number or letter on each ball. Throw a ball in the air and shout out what is written on the ball before you catch it.

# HAN AND LEIA ARE CAPTURED

**D**arth Vader had recruited bounty hunters to track down the *Millennium Falcon*. Suddenly, it was spotted on the sensors. Han and Chewie flew expertly, dodging asteroids and Imperial laser fire. They tried to make the jump to lightspeed but the transfer circuits weren't working. Thinking quickly, Han turned the *Falcon* around to face the Imperial Star Destroyer and flew past them, close to the surface. The Imperial scopes lost sight of the *Falcon* . . . Han had hidden the *Falcon* on the Imperial ship itself – so close, the sensors couldn't detect them!

The plan was to wait until the Imperial ship got rid of their rubbish, so the *Falcon* could float away amongst the debris undetected. Han searched for a safe port nearby and saw that his old friend, Lando Calrissian, was now the leader of Cloud City, a mining station and colony floating above the planet Bespin. They

> ## "I WANT THEM ALIVE."
> **DARTH VADER**

detached the *Falcon* from the Star Destroyer and set a course for Cloud City – not realising that they were being followed by the cunning and dangerous bounty hunter Boba Fett.

When they landed they were met by Lando, who seemed happy to see his old friend. But Leia did not trust Lando and was sure that something strange was going on in the city.

Lando invited everyone for refreshment . . . but it was a trap. Darth Vader and Boba Fett were waiting for them. Darth Vader imprisoned them all, but took Han for special testing – he was a test run for carbonite freezing to ensure it was safe for Luke. Boba Fett would take Han, frozen in carbonite, to the intergalactic gangster Jabba the Hutt, to pay for Han's debts.

# REBEL IN CARBONITE

Han has been frozen in carbonite and now it's Luke's turn. As he gets lowered into the freezing solution, solve these anagrams to get him out.

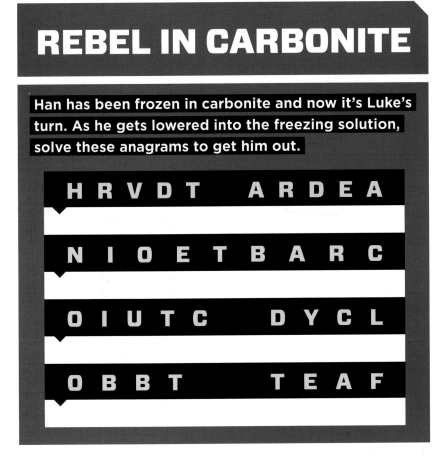

HRVDT ARDEA

NIOETBARC

OIUTC DYCL

OBBT TEAF

# MILLENNIUM FALCON QUIZ

**Could you drive the *Millennium Falcon* - the fastest hunk of junk in the galaxy?**
**Take this quiz and find out if you can get your licence.**

**Which two weapons does the *Falcon* carry?**

A. Light laser cannon
B. Superlaser torpedo
C. Twin quad laser cannons
D. Super-charged missile

**It is illegal for a ship of the *Falcon*'s size to carry as many weapons as it has on board.**

☐ TRUE   ☐ FALSE

**What type of ship is the *Millennium Falcon*?**

A. YT-1300 light freighter
B. AA-9 Coruscant freighter
C. Venturer-class freighter
D. Naboo freighter

**How did Han Solo become the owner of the *Millennium Falcon*?**

A. He won in in a game of sabacc from Lando Calrissian
B. He found it abandoned on Tattooine
C. He built it himself
D. He beat Jabba the Hutt at an arm-wrestle and won it as a prize

## What did you score?

If you think you need to take any sort of quiz or own a licence to own and drive the *Millennium Falcon*, then this is not the ship for you!

INTEL: *MILLENNIUM FALCON*

# A DESPERATE STRUGGLE

**R**eset the system for Skywalker and make sure he finds his way here," said Vader.

Luke was searching for Leia and Han. He found his way to the carbon-freezing chamber ... where Darth Vader was waiting .

"The force is with you, young Skywalker. But you are not a Jedi yet," said Vader.

Luke walked towards Vader and drew his lightsaber. The two began to duel.

"Only your hatred can destroy me," taunted Vader. Luke fought back and pushed him off a platform. Vader used the Force to throw different objects at Luke, until one broke a window and Luke was sucked out into the tall hollow of the building. He managed to catch the edge of a platform and pulled himself up.

On the narrow ledge outside, Luke struck Vader on his arm – but in retaliation Vader chopped off Luke's lightsaber-wielding hand.

"Don't make me destroy you," warned Vader. "Join me and I can complete your training."

> **"YOU MUST JOIN ME OR DIE."**
> DARTH VADER

"I'll never join you," shouted Luke angrily.

"Obi-Wan never told you what happened to your father," said Vader.

"He told me enough. He told me you killed him," replied Luke.

"No, Luke. I am your father."

Luke screamed out in anguish.

"You can destroy the Emperor, he has foreseen this. Join me, and we can rule the galaxy!"

Luke looked at Vader and then down at the vast drop below him. He let go and fell.

Luke was soon sucked into another pipe and he slid all the way down until he was hanging on an aerial at the bottom of the cloud city. Desperately, he called out for help.

Leia, meanwhile, with the help of Lando, had escaped on the *Falcon*. She heard Luke's call and turned back to rescue him.

# USE THE FORCE!

**How many times can you find the word 'Force' written in the grid below?**

| E | F | O | C | E | F | O | R | C | F | F | O | R | C | F |
|---|---|---|---|---|---|---|---|---|---|---|---|---|---|---|
| C | F | E | F | F | E | F | F | O | O | E | C | F | F | E |
| C | E | C | R | O | F | F | C | F | E | C | R | O | F | O |
| F | O | R | F | C | O | F | E | C | R | O | R | C | C | F |
| O | E | F | O | R | C | E | F | C | F | C | R | C | E | E |
| R | C | E | C | F | E | O | F | E | E | F | O | R | C | F |
| F | R | E | R | R | R | E | F | O | R | C | E | R | F | F |
| E | O | E | F | C | F | C | F | R | R | F | O | E | O | R |
| F | F | R | E | R | C | R | C | O | R | C | C | C | E | C |
| O | C | E | C | F | E | E | C | R | O | F | E | R | O | E |
| F | F | R | F | R | R | F | F | R | E | C | C | O | C | F |
| O | R | O | O | F | E | E | C | R | O | F | C | F | E | F |
| F | R | F | R | F | F | O | R | C | E | C | O | F | F | E |

FACT FILE:
**The Emperor**

**Name:** Darth Sidious, Senator Palpatine
**Species:** Human
**Home planet:** Naboo
**Little known fact:** His entire life was the culmination of a thousand year plan to overthrow the Republic and Jedi Order from within
**Skills:** The full power of the dark side of the Force, including Force lightning
**Weapons:** Lightsaber (red)

# THE PATH TO THE DARK SIDE

**Two paths lead to the dark side where you will become a Sith Lord, only one will lead you to Luke and the way of the Jedi. Can you find the right path to the Jedi-in-training?**

START

A

B

C

# SITH LORDS:
## ANCIENT ORDER OF THE DARK SIDE

### "AN INDIVIDUAL MAY DIE, BUT THE SITH ARE ETERNAL."

The Sith began thousands of years ago, when a rogue Knight embraced the dark side of the Force and was cast out by his fellow Jedi. He quickly gained a following and the Sith Order was born. Inevitably this Order self-destructed after years of in-fighting and power-stealing, making it easy for the Jedi to wipe them out.

This lead a survivor, Darth Bane, to restructure the cult, so that there could only be two – a master, and an apprentice – at any one time. When the apprentice had learned all they could from the master, it was their duty to kill the master and take an apprentice of their own, in order to ensure the continuing strength of the cult.

## THE SITH CODE

*PEACE IS A LIE.*

*THERE IS ONLY PASSION.*

*THROUGH PASSION I GAIN STRENGTH.*

*THROUGH STRENGTH I GAIN POWER.*

*THROUGH POWER I GAIN VICTORY.*

*THROUGH VICTORY MY CHAINS ARE BROKEN.*

*THE FORCE SHALL SET ME FREE.*

# THE RULE OF TWO

Darth Bane enforces the rule of two. Use the code to work out what he says.
Two letters are missing, can you fill in the gaps?

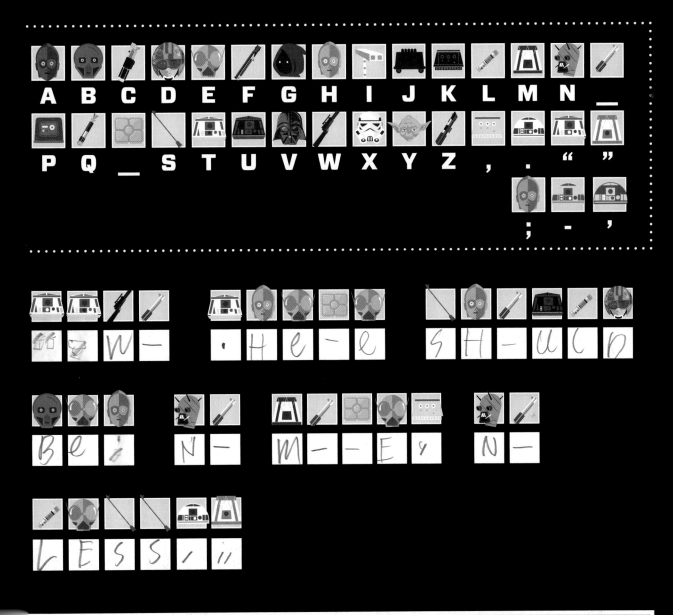

A B C D E F G H I J K L M N _
P Q _ S T U V W X Y Z , . " "
; – '

THE W_ _HE_E SH_ULD

BE_ N_ M_E&_ N_

LESS/_

---

# JABBA'S FAVOURITE DECORATION

**"I LIKE CAPTAIN SOLO WHERE HE IS."**
**JABBA THE HUTT**

Luke sent C-3PO and R2-D2 to Jabba the Hutt, a large slug-like creature who was a dangerous gangster, in exchange for Han's freedom. Jabba laughed; he did not believe that Luke was a Jedi and besides, he didn't want to give up his favourite ornament – Han frozen in carbonite was hanging on his wall.

Later, a bounty hunter arrived to hand Chewie over to Jabba for a reward. Chewie was taken to a cell. But later that night the bounty hunter crept into Jabba's lair and freed Han. As Han fell to the ground, he realised the bounty hunter was Leia! At that moment, a curtain drew back revealing Jabba. Han and Leia were arrested.

The next day, Luke himself arrived. He warned Jabba that he should accept what he had offered or be destroyed. In response, Jabba opened a trap door beneath Luke's feet and he dropped into a pit.

Inside the pit was a terrifying rancor with a mouth full of sharp teeth, which leapt to attack Luke. The exit was a dead end, and as the rancor came closer, Luke saw a switch for a heavy metal door, he threw a rock at it and it closed on the beast, killing it.

Luke and Han were dragged before Jabba again. He told them that they were to be taken on Jabba's floating barge to the Dune Sea and cast into the mouth of the Sarlacc, which would slowly digest them over the next thousand years.

As they were about to be pushed into the Sarlacc's jaws, Luke managed to jump into the air and catch his lightsaber, which R2 had ejected from a window on the hovering barge. With the help of Lando, who had disguised himself as one of Jabba's guards, they fought Jabba's men and took control.

**Name:** Jabba Desilijic Tiure
**Species:** Hutt
**Home planet:** Nal Hutta
**Little known fact:** Jabba is a hermaphrodite, which means he is both male and female
**Skills:** Ruthless crime-lord whose influence stretches for light-years across the galaxy
**Weapon:** An army of fiercely-loyal henchmen and bounty hunters

**TEST YOUR INTEL:**
**What planet does Jabba the Hutt live on?**

# KNOW YOUR ENEMY

**When faced with an enemy as dangerous as Jabba the Hutt, it pays to know the facts. Next to each fact is a sum, the only true facts have an answer that ends in '5' – circle the true facts.**

**1) 17 + 8 =**

Jabba keeps a pet rancor in a hidden pit.

**2) 15 + 2 =**

Jabba is a female Hutt.

**3) 9 - 4 =**

Jabba is known as 'The Bloated One', but never to his face.

**4) 27 - 2 =**

Jabba's sidekick is called Bib Fortuna.

**5) 8 + 20 =**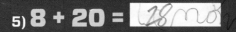

Jabba has two small legs hidden underneath his large body.

**6) 9 x 2 =**

Jabba has never employed Han Solo to smuggle for him.

# A FATAL ERROR?

The Rebels gathered for a briefing. They had new information that pinpointed the exact position of the new Death Star – and the weapon systems were not yet operational. The Imperial fleet were scattered through the galaxy in an attempt to find and destroy all Rebel bases, leaving the battle station unprotected. Best of all, the Emperor himself was aboard the Death Star to oversee the final stages of construction.

Admiral Ackbar went onto explain that the Death Star was orbiting the forest moon of Endor, and that it had a strong energy shield, generated from the moon itself. The shield needed to be deactivated before any attack could take place. The Rebel fighters would then take out the main reactor. General Lando Calrissian, who had joined the Rebel Alliance, would lead the fighter attack.

The Rebels had stolen a small Imperial ship

**"I WILL DEAL WITH THEM MYSELF."**
**DARTH VADER**

and would smuggle a small team down to the surface of the moon to deactivate the shield generator. The team who would undergo this dangerous mission would be led by General Solo, along with Chewie, Leia and Luke.

Han reluctantly gave the *Millennium Falcon* to Lando as long as he promised to return her without a scratch. Han and his crew climbed aboard the stolen Imperial ship and set off for the moon's surface.

As Han piloted the stolen Imperial ship, he gave the Death Star command the pass code. Luke sensed that Vader was aboard the station, and Vader sensed Luke's presence too. Vader gave the command to lower the shield and let the ship land – he would deal with the rebel team himself on the moon's surface.

# UNDER CONSTRUCTION

The Empire are constructing their second battle station. If you were to build a space station, what would it look like? **Draw it below!**

THE DEATH STAR I

NAME YOUR SPACE STATION:

## FACT FILE:
### Stormtroopers

**Species:** Clones of Jango Fett and elite Human troops drawn from the worlds of the Empire
**Home planet:** Various
**Little known fact:** In the early drafts of *Star Wars*, stormtroopers carried lightsabers, and there were female stormtroopers
**Skills:** The Empire's crack troops, the Stormtrooper Corps are the galaxy's most highly-trained fighting force
**Weapon:** Blaster rifles, thermal detonators, and many vehicles including AT-AT walkers

# DECODING YODA

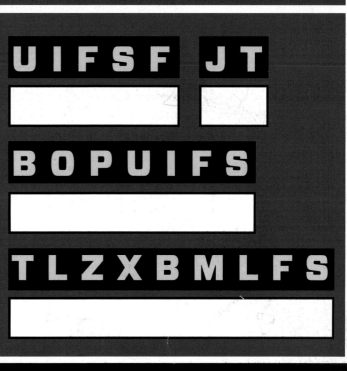

The letters for Yoda's final words to Luke have either all been shifted to the letter before or the one after the actual letter in the alphabet. Use the Force to work out which and then decode Yoda's final words.

| U I F S F | J T |
|-----------|-----|
|           |     |

**B O P U I F S**

**T L Z X B M L F S**

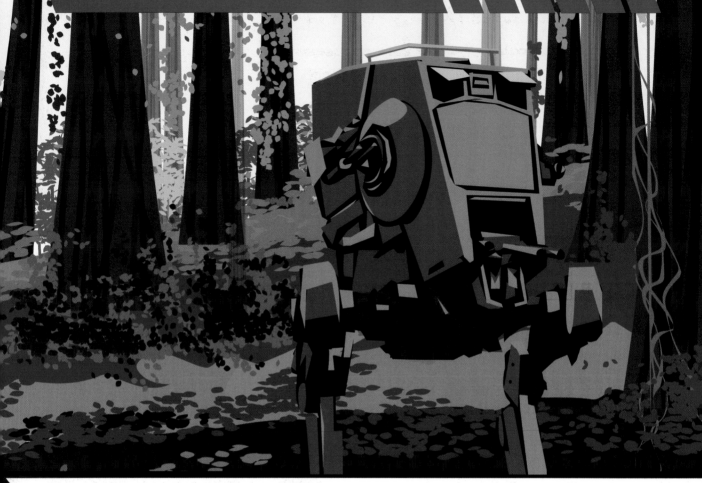

# THE REBEL ASSAULT

The Rebel team landed on the moon and set off to deactivate the shield – but were caught in a trap by a race of small, furry bear-like creatures called Ewoks. The Ewoks surrounded them, but as soon as they saw C-3PO, they started worshipping him! "Why don't you use your divine influence and get us out of this, 3PO?" asked Han, sarcastically.

"I beg your pardon, General Solo, but it's against my programming to impersonate a deity," replied C-3PO. So the Ewoks tied them up and carried them back to their village.

Back at the village, Luke told C-3PO to tell the Ewoks that if they don't let his friends go, he would get angry and use his magic powers. When the Ewoks didn't free them, Luke used the Force and made C-3PO float through the air. The Ewoks set everyone free and agreed to help the Rebels fight the stormtroopers on the moon.

Later, Luke told Leia that he must face Vader,

## "I KNOW THERE IS GOOD IN YOU."
**LUKE SKYWALKER**

his father, alone and that if he didn't come back she would be the only hope for the Alliance.

"Luke, don't talk that way! You have powers I could never have," said Leia.

"You're wrong, Leia. You have that power too. The Force is strong in my family. My father has it, I have it . . . my sister has it."

Leia looked shocked but realised that somehow she had known this all along.

"There's good in Vader, Leia, I can save him and turn him back to the good side," said Luke.

Darth Vader's ship landed near the shield generator, and Luke went alone to meet him.

"The Emperor has been expecting you," said Vader. "You don't know the power of the dark side. The Emperor will show you the true nature of the Force."

# EWOK DIRECTIONS

The Ewoks have agreed to show Luke, Leia, Han and the droids the way to the shield generator. Follow the key to help them reach their destination.

▼ START

| A | B | A | A | A | A | B | B | D | A |
|---|---|---|---|---|---|---|---|---|---|
| D | A | B | D | C | B | B | B | D | B |
| D | C | B | D | B | B | B | B | C | D |
| C | B | B | D | C | C | B | B | A | B |
| B | C | C | A | D | D | B | C | D | B |
| B | D | B | A | D | A | B | C | D | B |
| A | A | A | A | D | D | A | A | D | B |
| D | C | B | A | A | B | B | C | C | C |
| D | B | C | C | D | A | A | B | D | C |
| C | A | D | B | B | C | B | A | A | A |

A = RIGHT
B = DOWN
C = LEFT
D = UP

▶ FINISH

## FACT FILE:
## Ewoks

**Species:** Ewok
**Home planet:** The forest moon of Endor
**Little known fact:** The Ewoks are never referred to by name during Episode VI or the credits
**Skills:** Fierce fighters who use the forest to stalk and trap their enemies. The Imperial stormtroopers underestimated the furry little warriors
**Weapon:** Spears, slings and a variety of traps and snares

# PICTURE CLUES

It's likely that you can't speak Ewokese (unless you are fluent in over six million forms of communication like C-3PO), but do you know what words or phrases these pictures are showing?

**1**

GIVE GET
GIVE GET
GIVE GET
GIVE GET

**2**

MILONELION

**3**

PRO/
MISE

**4**

CHANCE CHANCE CHANCE CHANCE

# THE PROPHECY IS FULFILLED

**A**board the Death Star, Vader took Luke before the Emperor.

"Your friends are walking into a trap. They'll find that the fire power of this station is quite operational," gloated the Emperor. "You want your lightsaber, don't you? Take it, I am unarmed. Use it. With each passing moment, your anger makes you more my servant."

The Emperor then gave the order for the Death Star to destroy the Rebel fleet with its superlaser. In desperation, Luke took up his lightsaber and attacked Vader – but then took control of his feelings.

"I will not fight you, father," he said.

"Your feelings betray you. If you will not turn to the dark side, perhaps your sister will..."

Luke, full of anger, attacked Vader again, until finally he cut off Vader's lightsaber hand.

"Good," laughed the Emperor, "Your hate has made you powerful. Now, fulfill your destiny and take your father's place at my side."

## "I WILL NOT FIGHT YOU, FATHER"
**LUKE SKYWALKER**

"Never," he told the Emperor as he threw away his lightsaber. "I'll never turn to the dark side. I am Jedi, like my father before me."

The Emperor attacked Luke with Force Lightning. Luke cried out for help, "Father, please!" Vader could watch no more; he picked up the Emperor and cast him into a shaft, destroying him.

Han's team had succeeded in lowering the shield, and it would not be long before the Death Star was destroyed. But Darth Vader had been mortally wounded by the Emperor's Force Lightning. "Go my son. Leave me," he said.

"I can't leave – I need to save you," said Luke.

With his last breath, Anakin told Luke, "You already have."

Luke and the *Millennium Falcon* escaped just before the Death Star exploded.

# ANSWERS

## Page 9
### STAR-DOKU

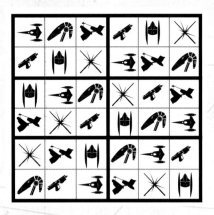

## Page 11
### GUNGAN WORD GAMES

**Duey** = two
**Ate-a** = eight
**Mesa** = I, I am, me, my
**Nutsen** = crazy
**Machineeks** = Droids or machines
**Ex squeezee me** = Excuse me
**Mesa greeting. In peles mesa comen** = Greetings, I come in peace
**Fraidee frog** = Coward
**Mesa doen nutten!** = I'm not doing anything!

### I LOVE YOU!
Jar Jar Binks

## Page 13
### JEDI COUNCIL

1. No
2. Circular
3. Brown
4. Brown
5. False

### YOU MAY NOT TRAIN HIM
Clouded this boy's future is.

## Page 15
### THE RULE OF TWO

## Page 19
### WHO IS JANGO FETT?

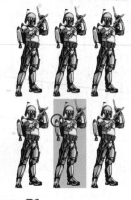

## Page 21
### ANAKIN'S PROMISE
I will be the most powerful Jedi ever

### CHASING DOWN THE FETTS

| 33 | 30 | 3 | 25 | 25 | 0 | 35 | 5 | 35 | 25 | 35 | 5 | 35 | 8 | 8 |
|----|----|----|----|----|----|----|----|----|----|----|----|----|----|----|
| 35 | 35 | 9 | 10 | 10 | 20 | 20 | 22 | 24 | 11 | 19 | 20 | 24 | 20 |
| 20 | 25 | 12 | 15 | 18 | 25 | 25 | 25 | 25 | 25 | 25 | 25 | 25 | 25 |
| 20 | 25 | 22 | 23 | 6 | 0 | 35 | 5 | 35 | 25 | 35 | 13 | 11 | 10 | 11 |
| 10 | 1 | 11 | 10 | 9 | 20 | 20 | 22 | 24 | 11 | 13 | 24 | 22 | 1 |
| 1 | 10 | 1 | 1 | 12 | 25 | 25 | 25 | 25 | 25 | 25 | 2 | 2 | 2 |
| 2 | 4 | 8 | 8 | 3 | 10 | 7 | 13 | 11 | 10 | 11 | 22 | 7 | 14 | 7 |
| 25 | 25 | 25 | 25 | 9 | 14 | 14 | 13 | 24 | 22 | 1 | 14 | 14 | 14 |
| 35 | 25 | 35 | 13 | 18 | 33 | 30 | 2 | 2 | 2 | 32 | 32 | 32 | 32 |
| 22 | 24 | 11 | 13 | 32 | 32 | 18 | 22 | 22 | 21 | 33 | 30 | 22 | 22 | 22 |
| 22 | 25 | 25 | 25 | 25 | 21 | 3 | 6 | 9 | 22 | 21 | 26 | 25 | 26 |
| 26 | 26 | 35 | 25 | 35 | 13 | 26 | 26 | 26 | 26 | 18 | 15 | 12 | 21 |
| 29 | 29 | 22 | 24 | 11 | 13 | 29 | 29 | 29 | 29 | 29 | 29 | 22 | 24 |
| 0 | 35 | 5 | 35 | 25 | 35 | 26 | 35 | 25 | 35 | 13 | 23 | 23 | 24 | 9 |
| 20 | 20 | 22 | 24 | 11 | 29 | 22 | 24 | 11 | 13 | 7 | 5 | 8 | 3 |

## Page 23
### A JEDI'S CHARACTER

### THE MASTER AND THE APPRENTICE

## Page 29
### GALACTIC WORD SEARCH

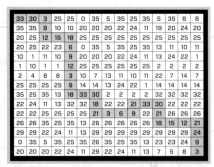

| B | S | A | M | T | C | W | E | L | S |
|---|---|---|---|---|---|---|---|---|---|
| U | G | A | I | L | P | S | N | Z | U |
| C | C | N | P | E | W | N | I | C | R |
| Q | M | A | M | Z | L | O | T | I | M |
| X | L | K | O | B | I | W | A | N | D |
| Y | W | I | S | D | I | U | P | F | B |
| V | O | N | L | N | C | A | L | J | F |
| A | K | A | D | M | A | F | A | U | S |
| A | A | U | M | K | X | T | P | U | S |
| B | C | C | K | I | T | H | O | J | G |
| G | Z | C | A | Z | D | V | Q | J | R |
| Y | K | G | A | B | E | A | B | U | I |
| C | E | T | U | B | W | Q | L | N | E |
| K | C | D | R | J | W | E | F | A | V |
| S | Q | G | J | Y | P | E | H | M | O |
| O | P | D | J | B | X | V | H | A | U |
| A | D | O | Y | J | C | R | P | C | S |
| D | A | M | I | D | A | L | A | Q | J |
| O | G | D | T | I | R | E | X | P | O |
| H | N | Z | A | Q | R | G | G | V | P |

**Page 31**

**GET GRIEVOUS!**

**CODE VICTORY**
Uncivilised

**Page 33**

**CHARACTER ANAGRAMS**
Mace Windu
Yoda
Obi-Wan Kenobi
Qui-Gon Jinn
Syfo-Dias
Ki-Adi-Mundi

**THE BIRTH OF DARTH VADER**
1

**Page 41**

**CHARACTER CLOSE-UPS**
**1.** C-3PO
**2.** Luke Skywalker (X-wing outfit)
**3.** Han Solo
**4.** Darth Vader
**5.** Obi-Wan
**6.** Stormtrooper
**7.** Chewbacca
**8.** Count Dooku

**Page 43**

**OBI-WAN SUDOKU**

| B | A | N | W | I | O |
|---|---|---|---|---|---|
| I | O | W | N | B | A |
| N | B | A | O | W | I |
| O | W | I | B | A | N |
| W | I | O | A | N | B |
| A | N | B | I | O | W |

**Page 47**

**DEATH STAR MAZE**

**Page 51**

**ARE YOU AS WISE AS YODA?**
**1.** Kashyyyk
**2.** *Millennium Falcon*
**3.** All Terrain Armoured Transport

**Page 55**

**REBEL IN CARBONITE**
Darth Vader
Carbonite
Cloud City
Boba Fett

**MILLENNIUM FALCON QUIZ**
**1.** A and C
**2.** TRUE
**3.** A
**4.** A

**Page 57**

**USE THE FORCE**
12

**THE PATH TO THE DARK SIDE**
C

**Page 59**

**THE RULE OF TWO**
"Two there should be; no more, no less."

**Page 61**

**KNOW YOUR ENEMY**
**1.** TRUE    **4.** TRUE
**2.** FALSE   **5.** FALSE
**3.** TRUE    **6.** FALSE

**Page 63**

**DECODING YODA**
There is another Skywalker

**Page 65**

**EWOK DIRECTIONS**

| A | B | A | A | A | A | B | B | D | A |
|---|---|---|---|---|---|---|---|---|---|
| D | A | B | D | C | B | B | B | D | B |
| D | C | B | D | B | B | B | B | C | D |
| C | B | B | D | C | C | B | B | A | B |
| B | C | C | A | D | D | B | C | D | B |
| B | D | B | A | D | A | B | C | D | B |
| A | A | A | A | D | D | A | A | D | B |
| D | C | B | A | A | B | B | C | C | C |
| D | B | C | C | D | A | A | B | D | C |
| C | A | D | B | B | C | B | A | A | A |

**PICTURE CLUES**
**1.** Forgive and forget
**2.** One in a million
**3.** Broken promise
**4.** Last chance